To Patricia
With love,

Lesley, James
q Elliott.

# Possum Magic

Omnibus
Books

For Chloë

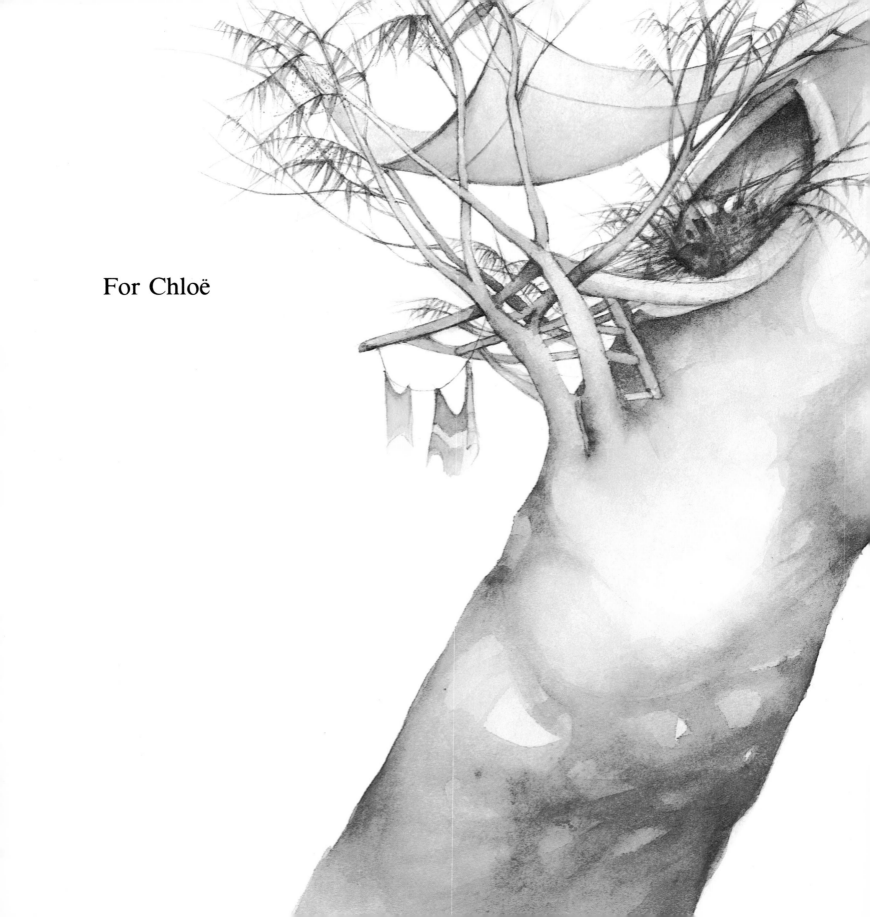

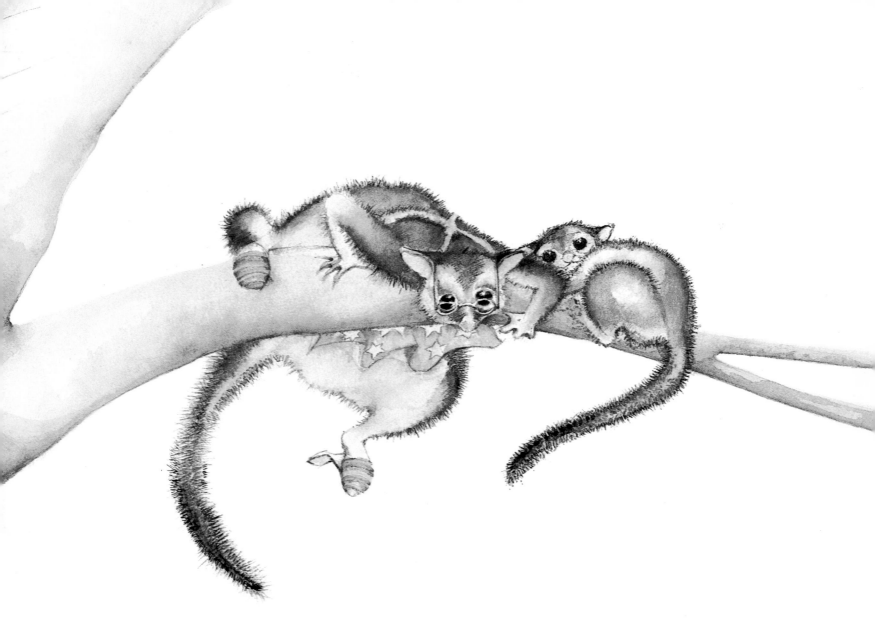

Once upon a time, but not very long ago,
deep in the Australian bush lived two possums.
Their names were Hush and Grandma Poss.

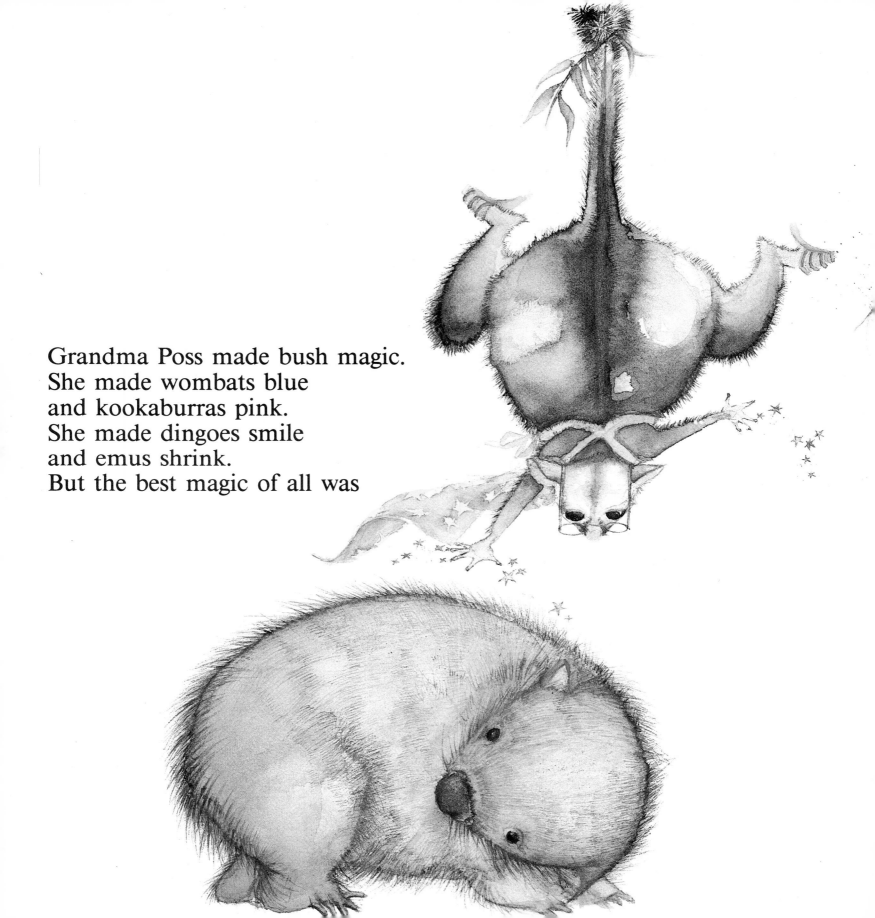

Grandma Poss made bush magic.
She made wombats blue
and kookaburras pink.
She made dingoes smile
and emus shrink.
But the best magic of all was

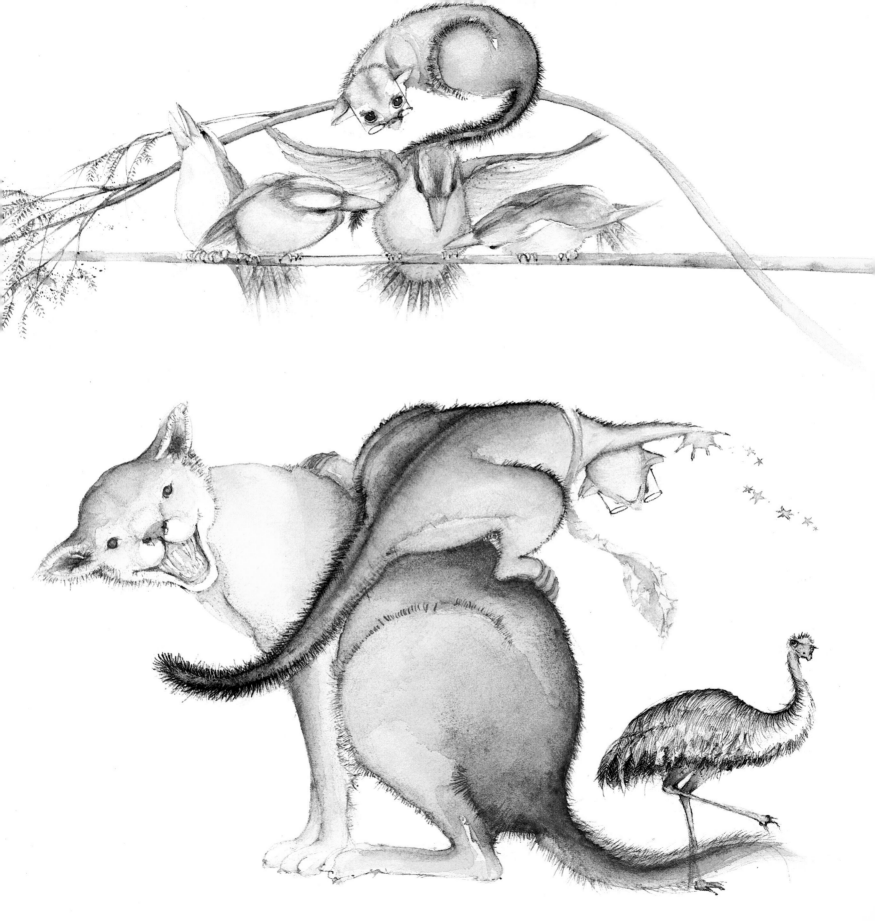

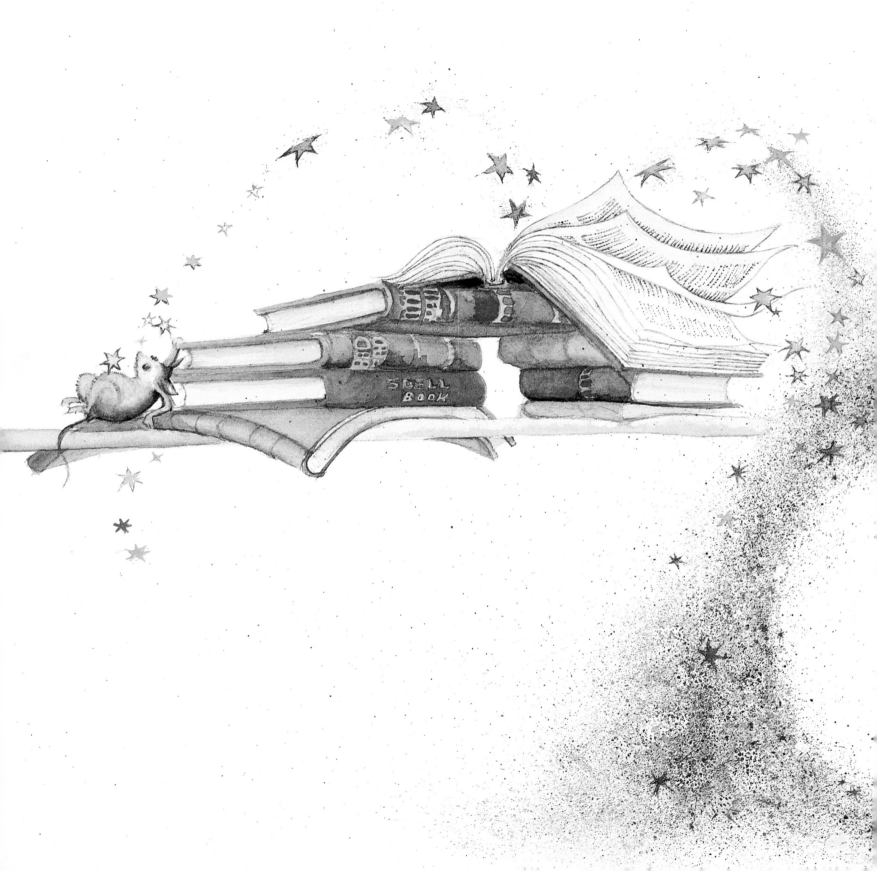

the magic that made Hush INVISIBLE.

What adventures Hush had!
Because she couldn't be seen she could be squashed by koalas.

Because she couldn't be seen she could slide down kangaroos.

Because she couldn't be seen she was safe from snakes,
which is why Grandma Poss had made her invisible in the first place.

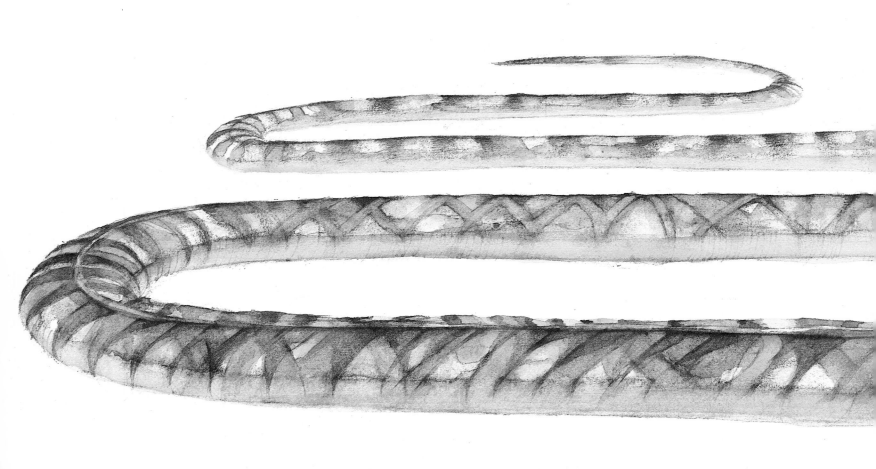

But one day, quite unexpectedly, Hush said,
"Grandma, I want to know what I look like.
Please could you make me visible again."
"Of course I can", said Grandma Poss,
and she began to look through her magic books.

She looked into this book and she looked into that.
There was magic for thin and magic for fat,
magic for tall and magic for small,
but the magic she was looking for wasn't there at all.

Grandma Poss looked miserable.
"Don't worry Grandma", said Hush. "I don't mind."

But in her heart of hearts she did.

All night long Grandma Poss thought and thought.
The next morning, just before breakfast, she shouted,
"It's something to do with food.
People food—not possum food.
But I can't remember what.
We'll just have to try and find it."

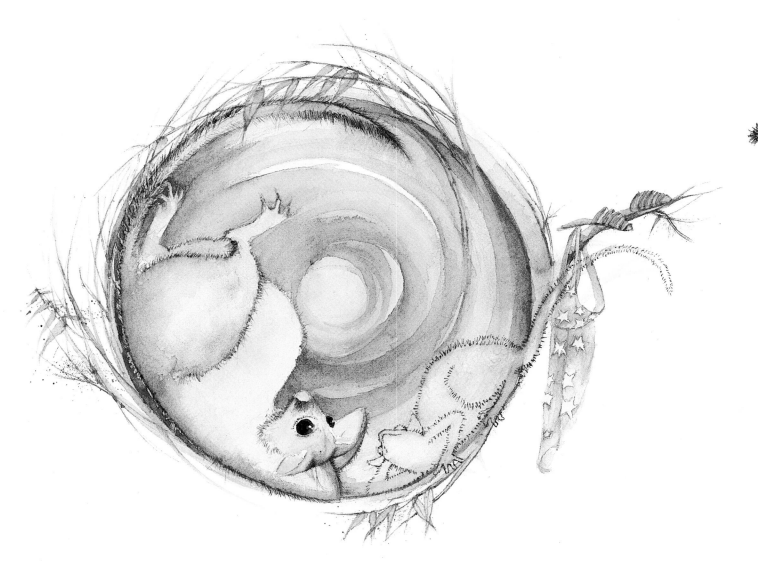

So later that day,
they left the bush where they'd always been
to find what it was that would make Hush seen.

They ate Anzac biscuits in Adelaide,
mornay and Minties in Melbourne,
steak and salad in Sydney
and pumpkin scones in Brisbane.

Hush remained invisible.
"Don't lose heart!" said Grandma Poss.
"Let's see what we can find in Darwin."

It was there, in the far north of Australia,
that they found a vegemite sandwich.
Grandma Poss crossed her claws and crossed her feet.
Hush breathed deeply and began to eat.
"A tail! A tail!" shouted both possums at once.
For there it was. A brand new, visible tail.

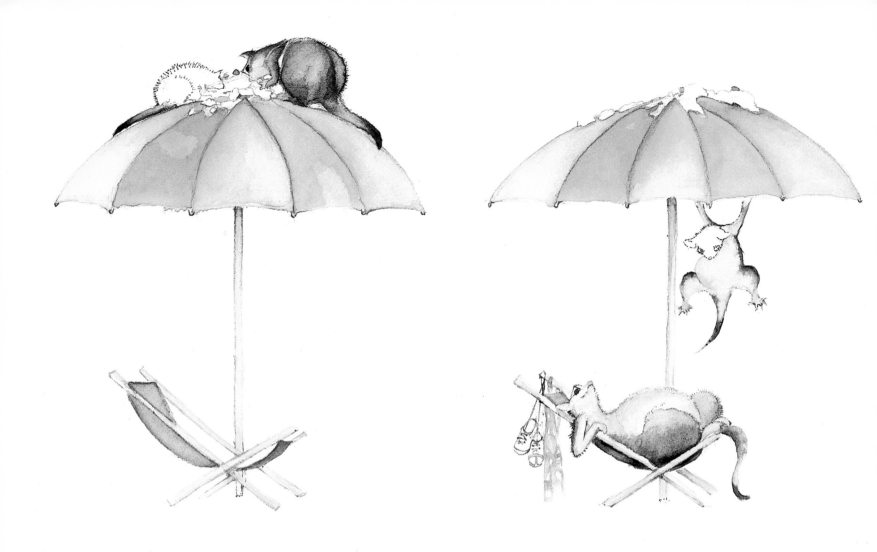

Later, on a beach in Perth, they ate a piece of pavlova.
Hush's legs appeared.
So did her body.
"You look wonderful you precious possum!" said Grandma Poss.
"Next stop—Tasmania."
And over the sea they went.

In Hobart, late one night, in the kitchens
of the casino, they saw a lamington on a plate.
Hush closed her eyes and nibbled.
Grandma Poss held her breath and waited.

"It's worked! It's worked!" she cried.
And she was right.
Hush could be seen from head to tail.
Grandma Poss hugged Hush, and they both danced
"Here We Go Round the Lamington Plate" till early
in the morning.

From that time onwards Hush was visible.
But once a year, on her birthday, she and Grandma Poss
ate a vegemite sandwich, a piece of pavlova and a half
a lamington, just to make sure that Hush stayed visible forever.

And she did.

Omnibus Books in association with Penguin Books Australia
First published 1983
Reprinted 1983 (five times)
Reprinted 1984 (ten times)
Reprinted 1985 (twice)
Reprinted 1986 (once)
Text copyright © Mem Fox 1983
Illustrations copyright © Julie Vivas 1983
Typeset by Modgraphic & Associates Pty Ltd, Adelaide
Printed in Hong Kong

National Library of Australia Cataloguing-in-Publication data:
Fox, Mem, 1946–    .
   Possum magic.

   First published: Adelaide: Omnibus Books, 1983
   For children.
   ISBN 0 949641 05 7

   I. Vivas, Julie 1947–    . II. Title.

A823′.3